Fae-Touched Vampires

Fae-Touched Vampires

Benjamin Blakeley

Published by Benjamin Blakeley, 2024.

FAE-TOUCHED VAMPIRES

First edition. February 21, 2024.

Copyright © 2024 Benjamin Blakeley.

ISBN: 979-8227684646

Written by Benjamin Blakeley.

Chapter One

Moonlight spilled through the dusty window, casting long, skeletal fingers across the bare floorboards. I lay sprawled on the cot, heart hammering against my ribs like a trapped bird. The dream clung to me, a tapestry woven with shadows and whispers, leaving behind a chilling residue of fear and wonder.

I squeezed my eyes shut, trying to recapture the fragments – a swirling vortex of emerald light, the scent of honeysuckle and ancient earth, a voice like wind chimes singing a mournful melody. Then, a flash of crimson, a clash of steel, and a scream that echoed through the ages.

A low groan escaped my lips. It wasn't the first time I'd woken bathed in sweat, haunted by these cryptic visions. But tonight, something felt different, a weight pressing down on my chest, a knot of unease twisting in my gut.

I sat up, the movement startling Aric, who lay huddled on the cot beside me. His sleep was always restless, plagued by the hunger gnawing at our undead hearts. But tonight, even though he stirred, his brow furrowed in concern.

"Another one?" he rasped, his voice gravelly with disuse. I nodded, unable to tear my gaze from the silver moonbeams dancing on the wall.

"Vivid," I whispered, the word tasting like ash on my tongue. "Too vivid."

Aric sighed, the sound a dry rustle in the stillness. He was my sire, my creator, the closest thing to family I had in this shadowed existence. He knew the burden I carried, the whispered rumors that swirled around me like smoke.

"Just another dream, Lyra," he said, his voice laced with forced reassurance. "They don't mean anything."

I scoffed, the sound harsh in the quiet room. "Don't mean anything? They feel real, Aric, like memories I can't quite grasp."

He sat up, his dark eyes searching mine. "They're just figments of your imagination, fueled by your..." he hesitated, choosing his words carefully, "...your uniqueness."

The word hung heavy in the air, a veiled reference to the whispers, the unspoken truth. I was different, even among our kind. Fae-touched, they called me, a creature born of an unholy union between vampire and faerie. An anomaly, ostracized and feared in equal measure.

"Maybe," I said, my voice tight with frustration. "But what if there's more to it? What if these dreams are trying to tell me something?"

Aric's gaze faltered. He knew my unease was justified. The prophecy, a cryptic verse passed down through generations, spoke of a Fae-touched vampire who would either unite or destroy our kind. A burden I shouldn't have to bear, a future I desperately tried to ignore.

Suddenly, a sharp rapping echoed through the stone walls, jolting us both from our tense silence. We exchanged a wary glance, the sound sending a shiver down my spine. Visitors at this hour were unheard of, especially not welcome ones.

Aric rose, his movements fluid despite his age. "Stay here," he commanded, his voice low and firm. "Don't open the door for anyone."

He grabbed his worn leather coat and slipped out of the room, leaving me alone with the gnawing fear in my stomach and the lingering echoes of my unsettling dream. Minutes stretched into an eternity, each creak of the old house amplifying my anxiety. Finally, the door creaked open and Aric reappeared, his face etched with worry.

"It's Markus," he said, his voice tight. "He says it's urgent."

Markus, the elder of the coven, rarely ventured into our secluded corner of the crypt. His visit could only mean bad news. My heart hammered a frantic rhythm against my ribs as I followed Aric down the narrow, cobbled passage.

We found Markus in the main chamber, a flickering torch casting grotesque shadows on the stone walls. His face, usually stoic, was etched with a grim urgency.

"Lyra," he said, his voice raspy with age. "We need to talk."

My breath hitched. The way he looked at me, with a mixture of fear and hope, sent a jolt of apprehension through me.

"What is it?" I asked, my voice barely a whisper.

He hesitated, then took a deep breath. "The prophecy," he began, his voice heavy with dread. "It seems... it may be coming true."

My blood ran cold. The whispers, the dreams, the fear – it was all converging into a terrifying reality. The prophecy, once a distant murmur, now loomed over me like a storm cloud, threatening to engulf me in its darkness. As Markus spoke, his words painted a picture of impending danger.

The air crackled with tension, the weight of Markus's words pressing down on the room like a physical force. He spoke of a growing unease within the vampire community, whispers of unrest stirring amongst the fae, and a cryptic message received from a secluded oracle, all pointing towards a brewing conflict.

"They believe you might be the key, Lyra," he finished, his eyes boring into mine. "The Fae-touched one spoken of in the prophecy."

A cold dread pooled in my stomach. The burden I desperately tried to ignore had materialized, a dark prophecy pinning me to a future I didn't choose. Fear threatened to consume me, but a spark of defiance ignited within.

"The prophecy also speaks of unification," I countered, my voice gaining strength despite the tremor in my limbs. "Perhaps there's another way, a way to bridge the divide and avert this conflict."

Markus's expression softened slightly. "Perhaps," he conceded. "But the path is fraught with danger. Are you willing to walk it, Lyra?"

The question hung heavy in the air, demanding an answer. The thought of wielding such power, of influencing the fate of both vampires and fae, was daunting. Yet, the alternative – letting fear dictate my fate, letting the prophecy unfold unchecked – was unthinkable.

I met his gaze, my resolve hardening. "I have no choice," I said, my voice echoing in the cavernous chamber. "These dreams, this... uniqueness... They mean something. I have to understand them, for my sake and for the sake of both our kind."

A flicker of pride danced in Markus's eyes. "Then you have our support, Lyra," he said, his voice regaining its usual authority. "But remember, the path you choose will have consequences. Be prepared to face them."

His words served as both a warning and a challenge. As I nodded, a surge of determination coursed through me. The whispers, the dreams – they weren't just figments of my imagination. They were a call to action, a destiny I couldn't escape.

The following days were a whirlwind of activity. Aric, despite his initial reservations, became my staunch supporter, training me to hone my senses and control the bursts of unpredictable magic that simmered within me. The elders, though wary, offered their grudging assistance, sharing forbidden texts and forgotten lore about the Fae-touched vampires.

Each revelation chipped away at the veil of secrecy, revealing a truth more complex than the simplistic good versus evil narrative whispered amongst the coven. The history was rife with conflict, yes, but also with alliances, with moments of fragile peace shattered by misunderstandings and power struggles.

The more I learned, the more the lines between vampire and fae blurred. Their magic echoed in my veins, their emotions resonated with my own. The prophecy, once a threat, started to feel like a responsibility, a chance to bridge the gap, to forge a new path.

But whispers of dissent reached my ears. Not everyone in the coven embraced my quest. Some saw me as a dangerous anomaly, a harbinger of doom. Others, blinded by fear and prejudice, advocated for my exile, even my elimination.

Their negativity fueled my resolve. I wouldn't let fear dictate my actions. I would face the challenge head-on, seeking answers not just within the dusty tomes and whispered warnings, but in the heart of the fae realm itself.

One moonlit night, under the watchful eye of Aric and a handful of trusted allies, I stood at the edge of the forbidden forest, the gateway to the fae realm shimmering before me. The air crackled with anticipation, the scent of blooming moon flowers thick in the air.

Taking a deep breath, I stepped forward, ready to confront the whispers, the prophecy, and my own destiny. The journey into the unknown, fraught with danger and uncertainty, had begun.

Chapter Two

The scent of mildew and decaying leaves assaulted my senses as I plunged deeper into the forbidden forest. Sunlight, filtered through a dense canopy of ancient oaks, dappled the forest floor in shifting patterns. It was both beautiful and unsettling, a stark contrast to the cold, sterile confines of the crypt that had been my only home for centuries.

Aric walked beside me, his silence a comforting presence. He understood my apprehension, knew the weight of the unknown pressing down on me. Yet, I also sensed a flicker of fear in his obsidian eyes, a fear not just for me, but for the potential consequences of our actions.

We moved with practiced stealth, our footsteps light on the moss-covered carpet. My senses, heightened by the magic thrumming in the air, picked up the rustle of unseen creatures, the murmur of wind through leaves, the distant gurgle of an unseen stream. It was a symphony of nature, a stark contrast to the muted hush of the vampire world.

Suddenly, a sharp prickle of energy surged through me, jolting me from my observations. My hand, clenched at my side, tingled like it was buzzing with electricity. Before I could react, a bolt of emerald light shot from my fingertips, illuminating the path ahead with an unnatural glow. A startled chirp echoed from a nearby tree, and I flinched, quickly extinguishing the errant magic. Shame and frustration burned in my gut. These uncontrolled outbursts were becoming more frequent, more powerful, and increasingly difficult to suppress. What if I lost control in the fae realm, where magic pulsed as naturally as breath?

"Easy there, Lyra," Aric murmured, placing a reassuring hand on my shoulder. "You're pushing yourself too hard."

"I have to," I retorted, my voice sharp with self-recrimination. "I can't control it, Aric. What if it happens again, in front of them?"

"They may not be as hostile as you think," he said, his voice laced with hope. "The prophecy... It could bring them hope too."

The word hung heavy in the air, laden with both possibility and risk. The elders had warned me of the fae's volatile nature, their ancient grudges simmering just beneath the surface. Yet, a sliver of doubt gnawed at me. Were they truly our adversaries, or were we blinded by generations of prejudice?

As we ventured deeper into the forest, the air grew heavy with a strange sweetness, unlike anything I'd ever encountered. The path narrowed, winding between colossal trees whose gnarled branches intertwined overhead, forming a verdant canopy that blocked out the sky.

Then, the silence was broken. A melodic chime, like wind chimes dancing in a summer breeze, echoed through the trees. It was accompanied by a chorus of unseen birdsong, a symphony of nature both enchanting and alien.

My heart hammered against my ribs, a mixture of anticipation and fear churning in my stomach. We were close. The gateway, the whispers said, was guarded by a magical barrier, invisible to the untrained eye.

Aric held up a hand, signaling me stop. From his frayed leather cloak he produced a small, delicate box containing several glowing green quartz stones. He whispered an ancient spell, and the quartz stone glowed softly and spun in his hands.

"The Veil of Illusions," he explained, his voice barely a whisper. "It will mask our presence from the guardians."

He pressed the stones to various points on the ancient bark of a nearby tree, each touch triggering a ripple of energy through the air. Slowly, a shimmering portal materialized before us, its edges shimmering with emerald light.

My breath caught in my throat. This was it. The bridge between two worlds, the threshold to a destiny I barely understood.

"Remember," Aric said, his gaze intense, "treachery can take many forms. Be on your guard, trust your instincts, and above all, don't hesitate to use your power if needed."

I nodded, the weight of his words settling on my shoulders. This was beyond a simple mission; it was a step into the unknown, a gamble with the future of both our kind.

Taking a deep breath, I stepped through the shimmering veil, stepping into the heart of the fae realm, leaving behind the familiar shadows of the vampire world and embracing the uncertainties that lay ahead.

The moment I crossed the threshold, a wave of energy washed over me, so potent it almost knocked me off my feet. The air tingled with magic, an omnipresent force woven into the very fabric of the land. Sunlight, filtered through leaves of iridescent hues, painted the forest floor in a kaleidoscope of colors. Flowers bloomed in impossible shades, their petals shimmering with an otherworldly glow.

The air was alive with the sounds of unseen creatures, chirps.

Chapter Three

The fae realm was an assault on the senses. Vibrant flora, alien yet captivating, bloomed in impossible colors, their sweet, cloying perfume heavy in the air. My skin tingled with the omnipresent magic, its energy buzzing beneath my fingertips. Unlike the cold, sterile magic of the crypt, this felt primal, untamed, echoing a rhythm deep within me.

Aric, usually stoic, seemed momentarily awestruck, his gaze sweeping over the fantastical landscape. Then, his shoulders tensed, and he drew me closer, his voice a low murmur.

"Stay vigilant, Lyra. This world can be beautiful and treacherous in equal measure."

We moved cautiously, following a barely discernible path that twisted between towering trees with bark that shimmered like moonlight. Every rustle of leaves, every flicker of movement sent a jolt of anticipation through me. It felt like entering a mythical tapestry, a dream come alive.

Suddenly, a flash of emerald light streaked through the undergrowth, followed by the high-pitched trill of unseen creatures. Fear, sharp and visceral, pricked at my skin. My hand instinctively reached for the hidden dagger Aric had given me, the cold metal reassuring against my palm.

"Calm yourself, Lyra," Aric whispered, his voice steady despite the tension in his posture. "They can sense fear."

Easier said than done. Every instinct screamed caution, yet a deeper purpose urged me forward. I yearned to understand this world, to connect with the magic that resonated so deeply within me.

As we ventured deeper, the forest changed. The sun-dappled path gave way to a dense canopy, sunlight struggling to penetrate the thick foliage. Shadows stretched long and menacing, and an unsettling silence had settled in, broken only by the occasional rustle of unseen creatures.

Then, a glint of silver caught my eye, peeking through the dense undergrowth. Curiosity battling fear, I knelt and brushed aside the leaves, revealing a half-buried stone archway. Its surface was intricately carved with symbols that pulsed with an ethereal glow, reminding me of the ancient texts I'd seen in the coven's forbidden library.

"A hidden entrance," Aric muttered, his voice tinged with awe. "This could be where the rumors lead."

With a shared glance of trepidation, we entered the archway. The passage beyond was narrow and claustrophobic, the air thick with the scent of damp earth and something faintly floral. We trudged forward, our footsteps echoing ominously in the stillness.

Finally, the passage opened into a hidden chamber, illuminated by an unseen source of pale light. Bookshelves, crammed with dusty tomes bound in leather and bark, lined the walls. An ornate table stood in the center, bearing an open scroll inscribed with symbols identical to the ones on the archway.

A sense of awe, coupled with a prickling unease, settled over me. This was a treasure trove of forgotten knowledge, a glimpse into a past hidden from both vampires and fae.

Aric approached the table cautiously, his eyes scanning the inscription on the scroll. "This language... it's ancient Fae, almost lost to time," he murmured, his fingers tracing the intricate symbols.

"What does it say?" I asked, my curiosity overwhelming my fear.

He frowned, his brow furrowed in concentration. "It speaks of a forgotten alliance, a pact between vampire and fae forged during a time of great peril. It mentions..." his voice trailed off, his eyes widening in shock.

"Mentions what?" I pressed, anticipation gnawing at me.

He looked at me, his gaze intense. "It mentions the Fae-Touched, Lyra. It calls them bridges, instruments of harmony between our two worlds."

My heart hammered against my ribs. Could it be true? Was this hidden library the key to understanding my own existence, my role in the prophecy?

Driven by an insatiable hunger for knowledge, I began exploring the shelves, pulling out dusty tomes and deciphering their faded script. With each page, a piece of the puzzle clicked into place. I learned of the ancient conflict, the animosity that festered between vampire and fae. But I also discovered whispers of a forgotten peace, a time when cooperation, not hostility, defined their relationship.

And most importantly, I learned about the Fae-Touched. Not as cursed outcasts, but as bridges, vessels of both vampire and fae magic, born to foster harmony between two warring factions. My eyes stung with tears, a mixture of relief and grief washing over me. I wasn't a monster, an anomaly. I was part of something bigger, something with the potential to rewrite the narrative, to heal the wounds of the past.

As I delved deeper into the texts, a chilling truth emerged. The prophecy wasn't just about unification or destruction.

It was about choice.

The words resonated within me, echoing the fear and hope already swirling in my gut. My existence wasn't predetermined, my path wasn't set in stone. The prophecy laid out the potential consequences, the stark reality of two contrasting futures, but the ultimate decision rested on shoulders.

Suddenly, a shadow flickered at the entrance of the chamber. Aric whirled around, his hand instinctively going to the sword concealed beneath his cloak. My own hand tightened around the dagger, adrenaline jolting through my system.

"Who's there?" Aric barked, his voice taut with tension.

Silence, save for the rustle of leaves drifting through the archway. Then, a figure emerged from the shadows, tall and slender with skin the color of twilight and hair like moonlit silk. Their eyes, emerald green and shimmering with an inner light, fixed on me with an intensity that stole my breath.

"Lyra," they said, their voice a melodic chime that resonated deep within me. "We've been waiting for you."

My mind struggled to comprehend. The whispers had mentioned guardians, protectors of these hidden archives. But this wasn't a warrior; this was a creature of ethereal beauty, their presence radiating power yet somehow inviting.

Before I could respond, Aric placed a hand on my arm, his voice low and urgent. "Stay back, Lyra. We don't know their intentions."

The fae being chuckled, a sound like wind chimes dancing in a gentle breeze. "Fear not, vampire. We mean no harm. We are the keepers of this knowledge, and we have watched you from afar."

"Watch me?" I echoed, suspicion battling the spark of curiosity dancing within me.

"Yes," they continued, their gaze unwavering. "We knew you would come. The prophecy has stirred, and you, chosen one, are its key."

Aric scoffed. "Prophecy? We don't believe in fairytales here."

The fae being's smile didn't falter. "Whether you believe or not, the truth remains. The shadows lengthen, and only the Fae-Touched can bridge the chasm before darkness engulfs both our worlds."

Their words sent a shiver down my spine. Darkness? Was this the true meaning of the prophecy? A looming threat bigger than just the simmering tension between vampires and fae?

The being held out a hand towards me, its palm glowing with an ethereal light. "Come, Lyra," they said, their voice laced with urgency. "There is so much you need to learn, so little time to prepare."

I glanced at Aric, seeking his guidance. His expression was conflicted, fear warring with curiosity in his eyes. But ultimately, he nodded, a silent acknowledgement of the weight of the situation.

Taking a deep breath, I met the fae being's gaze, resolving hardening in my chest. This wasn't just about me anymore. It was about understanding the prophecy, about forging a path that could avert the looming darkness. With trembling fingers, I placed my hand in theirs, stepping into the unknown, leaving behind the hidden library and the echoes of the past.

As we vanished into the shadows, the chamber fell silent, the ancient tomes waiting patiently for the next seeker of forbidden knowledge. The journey had just begun, and I, the Fae-Touched, was at its heart, walking a tightrope between two worlds, carrying the burden of choice and the weight of a potential destiny.

Chapter Four

Aric had returned shaken, his silence mirroring my own turmoil. He spoke little, his haunted gaze rarely leaving the flickering torch, as if replaying the meeting with the ethereal fae being over and over in his mind.

Suddenly, a sharp rapping echoed through the stone walls, jolting us both from our contemplative silence. My heart hammered against my ribs, dread painting cold fingers down my spine. Visitors at this hour were unheard of, especially unwelcome ones.

Aric exchanged a wary glance with me, his hand instinctively going to the sword hidden beneath his worn leather coat.

"Stay here," he commanded, his voice low and firm. "Don't open the door for anyone."

He grabbed his torch and disappeared down the narrow, cobbled passage, leaving me alone with the gnawing fear in my stomach and the chilling melody of the wind whistling through the broken window panes.

Minutes stretched into an eternity, each creak of the old house amplifying my anxiety. Finally, the door creaked open and Aric reappeared, his face etched with a grim urgency.

"It's Markus," he said, his voice tight. "He says it's urgent... and dangerous."

My breath hitched. The elder rarely ventured into our secluded corner of the crypt, especially not for trivialities. His visit could only mean bad news, news that likely intertwined with the unsettling events of the previous night.

Following Aric, I navigated the dimly lit corridors, every shadow seeming to harbor a sinister intent. We found Markus in the main chamber, the flickering torchlight casting grotesque shadows on the stone walls. His face, usually stoic, was lined with worry, his eyes flickering between Aric and me with a troubled glint.

"Lyra," he began, his voice heavy with concern. "We have received disturbing news. A hunter, notorious for targeting Fae-Touched, has been sighted near the borders of our territory."

A cold dread pooled in my stomach. Hunters were an ever-present threat, but the fact that this one specifically sought out Fae-Touched sent a shiver down my spine. Could they be aware of the prophecy? Did they know of my existence?

"They believe... they believe you might be their target," Markus continued, his voice hesitant.

The room spun around me, the weight of his words crushing. I wasn't just feared within the coven; I was hunted, seen as a monster even by those who should understand. A bitter laugh escaped my lips, devoid of amusement.

"Of course," I spat, my voice laced with anger and frustration. "Because being different in this world is a death sentence, isn't it?"

Markus remained silent, his gaze filled with sympathy and regret. He knew my pain, the ostracization I faced. But his silence offered no comfort, only fueled the anger simmering within me.

"What do they want with me?" I demanded, my voice gaining strength despite the tremor in my limbs.

"They believe you hold the key to some ancient power," Markus replied, his eyes downcast. "A power they intend to exploit, regardless of the consequences."

The fear threatened to consume me, but a spark of defiance ignited within. I wouldn't let them dictate my fate. I wouldn't become a victim of their prejudice and fear.

"I won't run," I declared, my voice ringing with newfound resolve. "I will understand this power, control it, and use it to protect myself, protect our kind."

Markus looked at me, a spark of admiration flickering in his eyes. "Then you have our support, Lyra," he said, his voice regaining its usual authority. "But remember, the hunter is cunning and ruthless. Be vigilant, trust your instincts, and above all, do not hesitate to use your power if needed."

His words served as a warning and a challenge. As I nodded, a surge of determination coursed through me. The hunter wouldn't break me. I would use this threat as a catalyst, an opportunity to unlock my power and find allies who wouldn't judge me for my uniqueness.

The following days were a whirlwind of activity. Aric, despite his initial disapproval, became my staunch supporter, helping me hone my senses and control the erratic bursts of magic that simmered within me. The elders, though wary, offered their grudging assistance, sharing forbidden texts and forgotten lore about the Fae-Touched.

Each revelation chipped away at the veil of secrecy, revealing a truth more complex than the simplistic good versus evil narrative peddled by the hunters.

with moments of fragile peace shattered by misunderstandings and power struggles. The more I learned, the more the lines between vampire and fae blurred. Their magic resonated in my veins, their emotions echoed in my own. The prophecy, once a threat, started to feel like a responsibility, a chance to bridge the gap, to forge a new path.

But whispers of dissent reached my ears. Not everyone in the coven embraced my quest. Some saw me as a dangerous anomaly, a harbinger of doom. Others, blinded by fear and prejudice, advocated for my exile, even my elimination. Their negativity fueled my resolve. I wouldn't let fear dictate my actions. I would face the challenge head-on, seeking answers not just within the dusty tomes and whispered warnings, but in the depths of my own power.

One moonless night, under the watchful eye of Aric and a handful of trusted allies, I stood in a secluded clearing, the air thick with anticipation. Aric placed a hand on my shoulder, his gaze reflecting the concern mirrored in the others' eyes.

"Are you ready, Lyra?" he asked, his voice low and serious.

I looked up at the star-dusted sky, drawing strength from the vastness above. "Ready as I'll ever be," I replied, my voice firm despite the nervous flutter in my stomach.

With a shared nod, they formed a protective circle around me, their presence a source of comfort and courage. Taking a deep breath, I closed my eyes and focused, pushing through the fear and doubt, summoning the magic within.

A low hum vibrated through me, growing stronger with each passing second. The air crackled with energy, and the leaves on the surrounding trees rustled as if touched by an unseen hand. My body tingled, an electric current dancing along my veins.

Then, with a burst of emerald light, my eyes snapped open. The world shifted, colors seeming brighter, sounds sharper. I felt connected to everything around me, the flow of life pulsing through the earth, the whispers of the wind carrying secrets on its path.

But the change wasn't just internal. The air around me shimmered, swirling with tendrils of emerald energy. My hands glowed with the same ethereal light, the power thrumming within me begging to be unleashed.

A gasp escaped one of the coven members, followed by hushed murmurs. Aric stood frozen, his eyes wide with awe and a hint of fear. For the first time, they were seeing the true extent of my power, and a flicker of uncertainty flickered in their gaze.

But I had no time for doubts. The hunter was close, according to the whispers I now understood. I had to learn to control this newfound power, not just for myself, but for the sake of those who stood by me and trusted in a different path.

The following weeks were a blur of intense training and experimentation. I pushed myself to the limit, exploring the boundaries of my abilities. I learned to channel the raw energy into shields, illusions, and even rudimentary healing magic. The frustration of erratic bursts gave way to a sense of control, a growing confidence in my abilities.

But every day brought news of the hunter's growing proximity. Reports of missing Fae-Touched from neighboring territories filtered through the coven, each story fueling my determination and stoking the flames of anger within me.

One night, as I practiced in the clearing, a chilling presence snaked its way into my senses. It was him, the hunter, drawing closer with each passing hour. Fear threatened to paralyze me, but the faces of my allies, their trust and encouragement, held me firm.

The clearing became my battleground. I conjured illusions, masking my presence, manipulating the shadows to my advantage. As the hunter drew near, I felt the predator's instinct within him, his focus laser-sharp, his senses honing in on my location.

A tense game of cat and mouse ensued. He would search, his steps heavy with determination, and I would shift, using every trick I had learned to stay hidden. The moon became my spotlight, casting long shadows that played into my illusions.

When he finally cornered me, exhaustion gnawing at my core, I knew it was time to confront him directly. My hand instinctively went to the hidden dagger, a cold comfort against the power surging within me.

"Who are you?" I demanded, my voice ringing with newfound power. "And why do you hunt the Fae-Touched?"

He didn't answer, his face hidden in the shadows. Only the glint of his silver blade reflected the moonlight, a chilling smile playing on his lips.

"You're different," he hissed, his voice raspy and laced with contempt. "An abomination, not to be trusted."

His words fueled my anger, but I channeled it into focus.

Chapter Five

The hunter lay crumpled at my feet, his eyes wide with disbelief. The clearing, once buzzing with anticipation, was now eerily silent, illuminated only by the waning moon. The metallic tang of blood filled the air, a stark contrast to the sweet scent of blooming night-lilies.

I stared down at him, the adrenaline slowly draining from my body, leaving behind a chilling emptiness. I had defended myself, protected those who trusted me, yet the victory felt hollow.

Aric knelt beside me, his hand on my shoulder, his expression unreadable. "You did well, Lyra," he said, his voice devoid of emotion. "But this changes everything."

He was right. The hunter's death would send shockwaves through the vampire community, further fueling the fear and prejudice surrounding the Fae-Touched. But the alternative, letting him harm me and countless others, was unthinkable.

As we disposed of the body, a sense of urgency settled over me. The hunter hadn't acted alone. He was part of a network, fueled by hatred and misinformation. I had to understand the bigger picture, find the source of their animosity, and prove that the Fae-Touched were not monsters, but bridges between our two worlds.

The whispers, the faint tendrils of energy I now sensed, offered guidance. They led me back to the hidden library in the fae realm, the knowledge it held promising answers.

Standing before the shimmering archway, I hesitated. Stepping back into the fae realm meant crossing a threshold, leaving behind the familiar shadows of the crypt and venturing into the unknown. But fear couldn't hold me back any longer.

Taking a deep breath, I stepped through the archway, the portal engulfing me in a wave of emerald light. The familiar vibrant flora greeted me, its alien beauty now tinged with a sense of foreboding. The air thrummed with magic, raw and untamed, yet strangely comforting.

Following the whispers, I ventured deeper into the forest, the path barely visible under the dense canopy. Shadows stretched long and menacing, and an unsettling silence enveloped me, broken only by the occasional rustle of unseen creatures.

Finally, the whispers coalesced into a distinct message, leading me to a hidden clearing bathed in moonlight. In the center stood a towering oak, its ancient branches twisted into an intricate canopy. Beneath it, etched on a moss-covered stone, was a symbol identical to the one inscribed on the archway.

As I approached, the air shimmered, and a wisp of ethereal light emerged from the symbol. It coalesced into a figure, tall and slender, with skin the color of moonlight and hair like spun silver. Their eyes, emerald green and shimmering with an inner light, locked onto mine.

"Lyra," their voice resonated within me, a melodious chime tinged with sadness. "You have returned."

"I need answers," I declared, my voice firm despite the tremor running through me. "Answers about the hunters, about the prophecy, about my place in this world."

The being smiled, a melancholic expression lingering in their eyes. "Answers you seek, within you lie," they said, their voice echoing with cryptic wisdom. "But the path is fraught with shadows and secrets, hidden depths only you can explore."

Frustration gnawed at me. "I need more than riddles," I pleaded. "Tell me where to go, what to do!"

They chuckled, the sound like wind chimes dancing in a gentle breeze. "Patience, young one. The journey unfolds one step at a time. Follow the whispers, heed the signs, and trust your instincts. They will guide you to the truth."

With a final wave of their hand, the being vanished, leaving me alone with the moonlight and the whispers swirling around me. Disappointment threatened to consume me, but the being's words resonated within me. Their cryptic message, though frustrating, held a kernel of truth. The answers didn't lie in someone else's hands, but within my own unexplored depths.

Drawing strength from the moonlight and the whispering energy of the forest, I resolved to follow their advice. I would explore the depths of my magic, hone my senses, and decipher the whispers, piece by fragmented piece.

The journey wouldn't be easy. Danger lurked in the shadows, prejudice simmered within the vampire community, and the prophecy loomed like a storm cloud overhead. But I wouldn't waver. I would embrace my uniqueness, wield my power with responsibility, and forge my own path, a path that bridged the chasm between two worlds and offered hope for a future free of fear and hatred.

As I started venturing deeper into the heart of the forest, the whispers grew stronger, weaving a tapestry of forgotten history, hidden alliances, and ancient magic. It was a daunting task, deciphering their fragmented messages, but with each step, I felt closer to understanding my own role.

PART TWO

Chapter Six

Moonlight painted the forest floor in silver strokes as I navigated deeper into its emerald embrace. The whispers, once faint hints, grew stronger, weaving intricate narratives of forgotten alliances and ancient betrayals. My head spun with their fragmented messages, yet each deciphered syllable ignited a flicker of understanding within me.

Suddenly, a rustle in the undergrowth sent a jolt through me. My hand instinctively went to the dagger hidden beneath my cloak, apprehension churning in my stomach. Yet, instead of the expected predator, a figure emerged from the shadows, bathed in the ethereal glow of moonlight.

Tall and lean, their silhouette was vaguely humanoid, yet cloaked in an otherworldly aura. Their skin shimmered with an iridescent sheen, their eyes glowing with an emerald light that pierced through the darkness, searching my own.

Fear warred with curiosity. Could they be another guardian, like the ethereal being at the library? Or something more sinister, drawn by the whispers echoing within me?

Before I could voice my question, the figure spoke, their voice a melodic chime tinged with amusement. "You are bold, venturing this deep into the heart of Elyria, where even shadows fear to tread."

The name sent a shiver down my spine. Elyria, the hidden realm of the fae, whispered in legends and forbidden texts. Was this being a fae creature, a denizen of that mythical land?

"Who are you?" I demanded, my voice hoarse despite my attempt at defiance.

"I am Kael," they replied, a hint of a smile playing on their lips. "Guardian of these ancient woods, protector of those who seek understanding."

Their gaze held mine, unflinching, yet strangely comforting. Perhaps it was the sincerity in their voice, or the aura of power I sensed emanating from them, but my apprehension began to ease.

"Understanding I desperately seek," I admitted, lowering my voice. "Answers about the hunters, the prophecy, and my own existence."

Kael tilted their head, their luminous eyes studying me intently. "A Fae-Touched, adrift in a world that fears what it doesn't understand," they murmured, their voice echoing with empathy.

My heart hammered against my ribs. The weight of their words resonated deep within me, confirming what I already knew, yet feared to acknowledge.

"Then perhaps you can help me," I whispered, hope flickering within me. Kael chuckled, the sound like wind chimes dancing in a summer breeze. "Help comes at a price, little one. Are you willing to pay for it?"

My mind raced. What did they require? My trust? My loyalty? Or something more intangible, something rooted in the depths of my magical abilities?

"If it leads to answers," I declared, my voice firm despite the tremor in my core. "Then I am willing."

A satisfied smile curved their lips. "Follow me then," they said, turning and fading into the shadows. I hesitated for a moment, fear battling with resolve. But the hunger for knowledge, the need to understand my place in this unfolding drama, propelled me forward.

We moved through the forest, Kael's presence a silent guardian beside me. The whispers grew louder, clearer, weaving stories of a past where vampires and fae walked hand in hand, united against a common foe. But also of betrayal, prejudice taking root, and the subsequent fracturing of the two realms.

Finally, we emerged into a hidden clearing, bathed in moonlight. In the center stood a towering crystal, its facets catching and refracting the light, casting dancing patterns on the surrounding foliage. As I approached, I felt a surge of magic, raw and potent, emanating from the crystal.

"The Heart of Elyria," Kael said, their voices echoing around me. "It amplifies the whispers, unveils the past, but be warned, child, the truth can be a double-edged sword."

Hesitantly, I placed my hand on the crystal's smooth surface. A wave of energy pulsed through me, visions flooding my mind. I saw ancient alliances forged, laughter echoing through moonlit glades. But I also witnessed the seeds of discord down, whispers of distrust turning into venomous accusations. The images shifted, showcasing battles fought under blood-red skies, trust shattered, leaving behind an ocean of hatred and fear.

The visions were overwhelming, a whirlwind of emotions threatening to consume me. I staggered back, tears stinging my eyes, the burden of history weighing heavily on my shoulders.

Kael was by my side in an instant, their hand on my shoulder, grounding me. "Remember, child," they said, their voice gentle yet firm. "The past, though painful, shapes the present. But it does not dictate the future."

Their words ignited a spark of hope within me. The future wasn't preordained; it was a tapestry woven with choices, with actions, with the courage to break free from the shackles of prejudice.

"What can I do?" I asked, my voice choked with emotion but my gaze resolute. "How can I bridge the chasm between our worlds, rewrite the narrative of hatred?"

Kael smiled, a hint of sadness clinging to their lips. "You, Lyra, are the bridge. Your unique heritage, your untapped power, they hold the key."

They gestured towards the Heart of Elyria, its light pulsing with renewed intensity. "This crystal can help you hone your abilities, unlock the true potential within you. But be warned, the path will be fraught with challenges, tests of your will and resolve."

Fear flickered within me, but it was overshadowed by a fierce determination. I wouldn't let fear dictate my journey. I would embrace my power, harness it for good, and become the bridge that united two divided worlds.

Looking at Kael, I saw not just a guardian, but a potential ally, a guide on this perilous path. "I accept your challenge," I declared, my voice ringing with newfound strength. "Teach me. Help me become the bridge the prophecy needs."

Kael's smile widened, their eyes glinting with approval. "Then let the training begin, Fae-Touched," they said, their voice echoing with power and promise. "Together, we may yet rewrite the destiny etched in whispers and carve a new path, one bathed in hope and understanding."

As the moonlight bathed us in its ethereal glow, I stood there, no longer a lost creature adrift in the shadows, but a warrior in the making, ready to embrace my unique identity and fight for a future where vampires and fae could coexist, not as enemies, but as allies. The journey ahead would be arduous, fraught with danger and uncertainty, but with Kael by my side and the echoes of hope resonating within me, I knew I wouldn't face it alone.

The whispers, once fragmented and cryptic, now held a different meaning. They weren't just messages from the past; they were a roadmap, guiding me towards a future where I could fulfill the prophecy, not as a pawn in a predetermined game, but as an agent of change, a warrior of both worlds, forever bound to the fate of Elyria and the vampire realm, forever walking the tightrope between two destinies.

And as I began my training under Kael's tutelage, honing my power and delving deeper into the secrets of the Heart of Elyria, I knew that the whispers were true. My journey had just begun, and the echoes of change were already reverberating through the night, carried on the wind, whispering promises of a dawn where fear would give way to understanding, and hatred would finally surrender to the light of hope.

Chapter Seven

Kael, my fae mentor, moved with the grace of a predator, their every step fluid and precise. I mirrored their movements, sweat trickling down my brow as I parried their attacks, the wooden sword singing in the still air. Days had turned into weeks under Kael's tutelage. My body, once awkward and hesitant, now moved with newfound confidence. The raw magic within me, once chaotic and unpredictable, responded to my will, forming shields, illusions, and bursts of energy that crackled around me. But this wasn't just about combat. Kael delved into the forgotten history of Elyria, sharing stories of a realm steeped in magic, vibrant and alive. He spoke of the ancient alliance with the vampires, broken by betrayal and misunderstanding, their world fractured for millennia.

Their lessons resonated within me, fueling my resolve to bridge the chasm, to rewrite the narrative etched in whispers and hatred. Yet, doubt still lingered. Could I, a creature ostracized by both worlds, truly foster peace?

Tonight, under the watchful gaze of the full moon, Kael led me to a hidden portal, shimmering with otherworldly energy. Its edges pulsed with an iridescent light, beckoning me towards a realm I'd only seen in forbidden texts and fleeting dreams.

"Elyria," he said, his voice tinged with awe. "The true source of your power lies within."

Fear danced in my stomach, but curiosity was a stronger pull. Taking a deep breath, I stepped through the portal, the world warping around me in a kaleidoscope of colors and swirling energy.

Then, silence. I emerged into a breathtaking landscape. Bioluminescent flora cast an ethereal glow, vibrant flowers blooming in impossible colors. The air itself thrummed with magic, its energy tingling on my skin.

"Welcome, Fae-Touched," a voice echoed around me, melodious and rich with power.

I turned to see a figure emerge from the shadows, tall and slender, with skin like moonlight and hair that shimmered like woven starlight. Her eyes, emerald green and filled with an ancient wisdom, locked onto mine.

"Queen Morwen," Kael bowed his head in deference.

The queen nodded, her gaze lingering on me. "Lyra," she spoke, her voice a caress. "Your arrival has been eagerly awaited."

My heartbeat quickened. The Fae Queen herself knew of me? Why the sudden interest?

"What do you want from me?" I asked, my voice firm despite the tremor in my core.

Morwen smiled, a hint of sadness lingering in her eyes. "Answers you seek, within you lie. But the path is veiled, shrouded in ancient prophecies and forgotten promises."

Her words felt cryptic, mirroring the whispers that guided me. Yet, there was a depth to them, a promise of revelation.

"Can you help me understand?" I pleaded, the weight of my destiny pressing down on me.

"Help you will find," she said, her voice tinged with amusement. "But the key lies in embracing your heritage, unlocking the true potential within."

She gestured towards a crystalline archway shimmering in the distance. "Beyond lies the Whispering Glade, where echoes of the past dance on the wind. Seek them, Lyra, and listen carefully. They hold the seeds of truth, the first step on your journey."

With a wave of her hand, she ushered me forward. Kael remained silent, his gaze unreadable. Hesitantly, I stepped through the archway, leaving him behind as I ventured deeper into the heart of Elyria.

The Whispering Glade was a sanctuary bathed in soft moonlight. Trees with leaves like living emerald whispered secrets as I walked, their voices weaving a tapestry of forgotten memories. Images flickered in my mind, fragmented visions of a past where vampires and fae coexisted, their magic intertwined in a dance of harmony.

But then, the images shifted, showcasing moments of discord, whispers of suspicion and resentment turning into accusations and open conflict. The final vision was brutal, a battleground stained with blood, trust shattered beyond repair.

Grief and anger welled within me, the weight of history heavy on my shoulders. How could I bridge this chasm of hatred when the past itself was stained with betrayal?

As if sensing my distress, a wisp of magic brushed against my cheek. A figure materialized before me, tall and ethereal, clad in shimmering moonlight. "Do not despair, young one," they said, their voice a melodic chime. "The past, though painful, shapes the present, but does not dictate the future."

It was the being from the library, the guardian who spoke of choices and paths not yet written.

"What can I do?" I whispered, tears stinging my eyes. "How can I mend what is broken, rewrite the narrative?"

Chapter Eight

Determination flickered within me, a spark of hope battling the despair threatening to consume me. The path wasn't easy, but sitting idle wouldn't mend the fractured relationship between vampires and fae. I had to prove myself worthy, demonstrate that the Fae-Touched weren't harbingers of doom, but potential bridges towards a brighter future.

As if summoned by my will, the shimmering archway reappeared, beckoning me back towards Morwen's presence. With a resolute stride, I stepped through, returning to the vibrant heart of Elyria.

Queen Morwen awaited me, her emerald eyes holding an ageless wisdom. "The Glade has spoken," she stated, her voice tinged with amusement. "It seems you hold the potential, Fae-Touched, but potential alone is not enough."

Her words, though seemingly dismissive, held a hidden challenge. I wouldn't back down. "Then test me," I declared, my voice firm despite the tremor of nerves. "Prove my worth, and I will do whatever it takes to fulfill the prophecy, to bridge the chasm that divides our worlds."

Queen Morwen smiled, a hint of warmth flickering in her eyes. "You speak boldly, child. But true strength lies not just in words, but in control, in understanding both the power you wield and the worlds you wish to connect."

With a wave of her hand, the world around me shifted. Lush greenery dissolved into a desolate wasteland, the vibrant magic of Elyria replaced by the oppressive shadows of the vampire crypt.

Fear tugged at my core. This wasn't just a test; it was a mirror reflecting the prejudice I faced both within my own kind and the fae realm.

Taking a deep breath, I suppressed the emotions threatening to overwhelm me. This was a test of control, not submission. Focusing on the magic within, I conjured a shield, deflecting the harsh winds that whipped around me.

Suddenly, a figure emerged from the shadows, its eyes glowing with predatory hunger. It was a vampire, but not one I recognized. Hunger radiated from it, twisting its features into a grotesque caricature of rage. The test had begun.

Aric's teachings echoed in my mind, his harsh but invaluable lessons on combat and control. Using a combination of illusions and bursts of energy, I kept the vampire at bay, avoiding unnecessary harm, my mind searching for an escape route, a solution that didn't involve bloodshed.

But the creature was relentless, its movements fueled by primal instinct. In a desperate attempt to break free, I channeled raw fae magic, a surge of emerald light blasting the vampire back into the shadows.

Silence descended, heavy and charged. Then, Morwen reappeared, her expression unreadable. "Impressive," she conceded, her voice devoid of emotion. "You wield power with raw strength, but true control lies in understanding."

The scene shifted once more, transporting me to a bustling marketplace in the heart of Elyria. Fae creatures milled about, their beauty mesmerizing but alien. Whispers followed me, laced with suspicion and fear.

"Look, the Blood-Kin!"

"A mongrel, not welcome here!"

The prejudice stung, mirroring the whispers and mistrust I faced within the vampire community. This wasn't just a test, it was a reflection of the very reality I sought to change.

Instead of reacting with anger or fear, I focused on empathy, connecting with the underlying emotions of the fae around me. Their fear stemmed from misunderstanding, from centuries of mistrust built upon past betrayals.

With newfound clarity, I spoke, my voice carrying across the marketplace, infused with both understanding and conviction. "I come not as an enemy, but as a bridge, a voice seeking unity between our worlds."

Silence fell, followed by murmurs of confusion, then curiosity. I shared my journey, my struggles, and my vision for a future where vampires and fae coexisted, not in fear, but in respect and understanding.

Gradually, the hostility abated, replaced by cautious interest. By the time Morwen returned, the marketplace buzzed with lively interaction, fae and Fae-Touched conversing animatedly.

She studied me, a hint of approval flickering in her eyes. "You showed not just power, but compassion," she acknowledged. "The first step on the path, Fae-Touched, but remember, the journey is long and fraught with challenges."

Relief washed over me, the tension slowly draining from my muscles. I had passed the first test, not just by showcasing my power, but by demonstrating my understanding of the delicate tapestry woven between both worlds.

Chapter Nine

Kael awaited me just beyond the archway, his form blending seamlessly with the shadows. "You did well, Lyra," he said, his voice a melodic chime devoid of emotion. "But the path ahead remains shrouded in mist."

His words echoed Morwen's cryptic pronouncements, leaving me yearning for clarity. "What am I supposed to understand?" I pleaded, frustration gnawing at the edges of my newfound confidence. "What does the prophecy truly mean?"

Kael remained silent for a moment, his gaze fixed on the moonlit canopy. "The prophecy speaks of a bridge, but its meaning extends beyond you, Fae-Touched. It hints at a larger shift, a convergence of destinies."

Intrigue sparked within me. "Whose destinies?"

He finally turned to me, his eyes shimmering with an ancient sorrow. "It's a history lost to time," he murmured, "a tale woven with alliances and betrayals, sealed with blood and forgotten promises."

Hesitantly, he began to weave a narrative, painting a picture of a past where vampires and fae walked hand-in-hand, their combined magic safeguarding both realms. Their power, born of contrasting yet complementary sources, created an impenetrable shield against a shadowy entity known only as the Devourer, a being of pure darkness seeking to consume all magic.

But whispers of discord poisoned the harmony. Jealousy festered, fueled by misunderstandings and power struggles. Accusations flew, mistrust seeped into their interactions, and eventually, a devastating conflict ripped them apart.

The world fractured, magic weakened, and the Devourer, sensing their vulnerability, surged forth. With their combined strength diminished, vampires and fae were forced to retreat, clinging to their separate realms, fear replacing trust.

The prophecy, Kael explained, hinted at a chance to rewrite this tragic past. It spoke of a bridge, a being born of both fire and moonlight, who would unite the divided realms and reignite their combined magic, finally vanquishing the Devourer.

My breath hitched in my throat. The prophecy wasn't just about me bridging the gap between vampires and fae; it was about forging an alliance to confront an even greater threat.

"But are they willing to believe in it?" I whispered, the weight of the revelation settling upon me. "After centuries of hatred, can they trust a Fae-Touched?"

Kael's expression remained neutral, yet a flicker of hope danced in his eyes. "It won't be easy," he admitted. "Prejudice runs deep, but fear, when potent enough, can forge unlikely alliances. The Devourer's shadow grows longer, and even the most entrenched hatred might give way to the instinct for survival."

The realization sent chills down my spine. It wasn't a hopeful revelation, but a pragmatic one. The future wasn't paved with rainbows and handshakes, but with desperate alliances born out of fear and shared threat.

He placed a hand on my shoulder, the touch surprisingly warm. "Your role, Lyra, is more than just a symbol of unity. You hold the key to reigniting their combined magic, the only force powerful enough to defeat the Devourer."

A wave of responsibility washed over me, heavier than any trial Morwen had thrown my way. I wasn't just a bridge; I was a weapon, a beacon of hope flickering amidst a storm of fear and hate.

Taking a deep breath, I met Kael's gaze, my voice trembling with newfound resolve. "Then let us begin," I declared. "Show me how to harness this combined magic, how to become the weapon the prophecy needs."

Kael smiled, a hint of warmth softening his features. "The journey will be long and arduous," he cautioned, "but you are not alone. We will walk this path together, Fae-Touched, for the fate of both worlds rests on your shoulders."

As the moonlight bathed us in its ethereal glow, I stood tall, the weight of destiny etched onto my soul. The whispers had transformed from cryptic messages to a chilling truth. The path ahead wouldn't be easy, but the alternative - succumbing to fear and allowing the Devourer to consume everything - was unthinkable.

I was the bridge, but the journey stretched far beyond mending fractured relationships. It was about uniting two ancient powers, forging an alliance fueled by desperation, and confronting an enemy that threatened to engulf everything in darkness. The fight for survival had begun, and I, the Fae-Touched, stood at the precipice, ready to step into the heart of the storm.

Chapter Ten

The training grounds buzzed with activity. Kael, his movements a blur of emerald light, parried my attack, the wooden sword singing as it clashed against mine. Sweat beaded on my forehead, my muscles burning, but a smile tugged at my lips.

Weeks had passed since my audience with Morwen, and my control over my Fae-Touched abilities had grown exponentially. Each session with Kael pushed me further, honing my skills and unlocking the hidden potential within.

But despite the progress, a shadow of unease lingered within me. Morwen's cryptic pronouncements and the veiled trials left me with more questions than answers. And the prophecy, its true meaning shrouded in ambiguity, weighed heavily on my conscience.

As I finished my final maneuver, disarming Kael with a flourish, he chuckled, his eyes twinkling with approval. "Impressive, Lyra," he said, sheathing his sword. "Your mastery grows with each passing day."

"But there's still so much I don't understand," I admitted, sinking down onto a moss-covered stone. "The prophecy, Morwen's motives, the growing unrest within Elyria..."

Kael's smile faded, replaced by a thoughtful frown. "Elyria is indeed on edge," he murmured, his gaze turning towards the distant spires of the Fae Palace. "Whispers of dissent fill the air, fueled by rumors of a manipulated prophecy, of hidden agendas from both the Queen and the vampires."

My heart skipped a beat. Could my audience with Morwen have sparked these whispers? Had my acceptance of her trials fueled the simmering distrust?

"What are they saying?" I asked, urgency creeping into my voice.

Kael sighed, running a hand through his shimmering hair. "They believe the prophecy, once a symbol of hope for coexistence, has been twisted by Morwen, used to justify her alliance with the vampires."

Anger flared within me. Morwen wouldn't manipulate such a sacred text for personal gain, would she? Yet, doubt gnawed at the edges of my trust.

"Is there any truth to these rumors?" I pressed, my voice barely a whisper.

Kael shook his head. "Only the Queen knows the true intent, Lyra. But whispers, once ignited, are difficult to extinguish, especially when fueled by resentment and fear."

My mind raced. Could the hunters' attack have been fueled by similar misinformation? Was I, unknowingly, a pawn in a larger, more sinister game?

Desperate for answers, I decided to seek them out myself. Avoiding Kael's watchful eyes, I slipped away from the training grounds, venturing deeper into the heart of Elyria.

The whispers grew louder as I delved into the bustling marketplace. Faces, once warm and welcoming, now held a flicker of suspicion. Groups huddled together, hushed voices carrying snippets of discontent.

"The Fae-Touched... a wolf in sheep's clothing."

"Morwen aligns with the Blood-Kin... what are they planning?"

The venom in their words stung, their distrust a tangible weight in the air. My optimism about bridging the gap between vampires and fae felt like a fragile dream, shattered by the harsh reality of prejudice.

Suddenly, a commotion erupted near the central fountain. A young fae, barely a child, her eyes blazing with anger, pointed an accusing finger at me.

"She's the one! The Blood-Kin! Morwen's puppet!"

Before I could react, a crowd gathered, fear morphing into aggression. Their shouts echoed in my ears, the words blurring into a cacophony of hate.

Panic threatened to consume me. This wasn't a training exercise, a controlled test. This was raw, unbridled animosity, and I was its target.

But fear wouldn't shield me. Drawing strength from the whispers within, I focused on calming the crowd, channeling empathy and understanding. "Listen to me!" I cried, my voice ringing with power. "I come not as your enemy, but as a bridge, seeking unity, not discord!"

Slowly, the shouts subsided, replaced by hesitant murmurs. I shared my story, my struggles, my vision for a future where understanding could replace fear.

It was a difficult conversation, filled with skepticism and distrust. But as I spoke, I saw glimmers of doubt in their eyes, the embers of prejudice fading under the light of genuine connection.

By the time the sun dipped below the horizon, the crowd had dispersed. The young fae girl approached me, her anger replaced by curiosity.

"Is it true?" she asked, her voice barely a whisper. "Can there be peace between fae and vampires?"

I smiled, placing a hand on her shoulder. "There can be," I said, my voice filled with newfound conviction. "But it starts with understanding, with listening to each other, with breaking down the walls of fear and prejudice, brick by fragile brick."

The girl's eyes widened, a flicker of hope igniting within them. As we walked away, I realized the whispers weren't just a burden, but a tool. They echoed the anxieties of both sides, revealing the cracks in the fragile peace. By addressing them, by fostering empathy and understanding, I could become the bridge the prophecy spoke of, not just between vampires and fae, but within each community itself.

The journey ahead would be treacherous. Morwen's hidden motives remained shrouded in mystery, and the seeds of dissent were deeply sown. But I wouldn't be swayed by doubt or fear. I had tasted the power of connection, the transformative potential of empathy, and I knew, with unwavering conviction, that this was the path I was meant to walk.

Days later, I stood before Morwen, my head held high, not as a supplicant, but as an equal. I recounted my experience, the whispers I'd heard, the fear simmering beneath the surface.

Her expression remained unreadable, her emerald eyes holding an unfathomable depth. "The whispers are fickle, child," she said, her voice a melodic chime. "They can be manipulated, twisted to suit one's agenda."

"But they also reveal truths," I countered, my voice firm. "They expose the raw emotions, the fears that fuel the discord."

Silence stretched between us, thick with unspoken tension. Finally, Morwen smiled, a hint of warmth reaching her eyes. "You have grown, Lyra," she acknowledged. "You see beyond the surface, hear the whispers not just with your ears, but with your heart."

Relief washed over me, tempered by cautious hope. Did this mean she acknowledged the truth in my words? Was she willing to work towards a solution?

"What happens now?" I asked, my voice barely a whisper.

Morwen's gaze drifted towards the distant spires of the Fae Palace. "The path ahead is fraught with uncertainty, child," she said, her voice echoing with an ancient wisdom. "But remember, the whispers are not your enemy. They are your guide, pointing towards the hidden truths, the path less traveled that may yet lead to the dawn of understanding."

With a final wave of her hand, she dismissed me, leaving me standing alone, the weight of her cryptic words settling upon my shoulders. The path ahead was indeed uncertain, but I wouldn't face it alone. I had the whispers, the growing trust of the fae people, and a newfound confidence fueled by empathy and conviction.

As I walked away, the whispers, once chaotic and disjointed, seemed to weave a new narrative. They spoke of unity, of collaboration, of a future where the Fae-Touched wouldn't be ostracized but embraced, not just as a bridge between two worlds, but as a symbol of hope, a testament to the transformative power of understanding and compassion.

The whispers, once a burden, were now my anthem, guiding me through the shadows, leading me towards a future where the prophecy wouldn't be a weapon of division, but a beacon of hope, a promise etched not in fear, but in the shared dream of a world bathed in the light of understanding, a world where vampires and fae could finally walk side by side, not as enemies, but as allies, united under one sky.

And as I stepped into the heart of Elyria, the whispers echoing around me, I knew my journey had just begun. The challenges would be many, the doubts would linger, but I would not falter. I was the Fae-Touched, the bridge between worlds, and I would carve my own path, a path paved with empathy, guided by the whispers, and illuminated by the unwavering hope for a brighter future.

PART THREE

Chapter Eleven

I wasn't there as an emissary of peace, but as a daughter returning home. Or at least, what remained of one.

Fear gnawed at the edges of my resolve as I approached the main chamber. Whispers and hushed accusations followed me like unseen wraiths. The prophecy, my connection to the fae, my very existence – they were all tinderboxes waiting for a spark.

And here I was, the spark itself.

Stepping into the chamber, I found Aric seated on his makeshift throne, his features grim, shadowed by flickering torches. The other Elders clustered around him, their expressions mirroring his disapproval.

"Lyra," Aric said, his voice laced with ice. "You return at an interesting time."

My throat tightened. The tension was suffocating, the air thick with unspoken judgment. "I bear news from Elyria," I managed, my voice barely above a whisper.

Aric snorted, a harsh sound that echoed in the silence. "News, or another fae trickery?"

His words stung, but I wouldn't let anger cloud my purpose. "No trickery," I replied, forcing my voice to remain steady. "I come to warn you of growing unrest, whispers of a manipulated prophecy fueling resentment towards vampires."

Silence descended, heavy and charged. The Elders exchanged wary glances, suspicion etched on their faces.

"And what role do you play in these whispers, Fae-Touched?" an elder with eyes like cold embers spat, his voice dripping with disdain.

My fists clenched at my sides. "I am a bridge, not a pawn," I declared, my voice ringing with defiance. "I seek understanding, not conflict."

Their laughter, cold and humorless, shattered the fragile silence. "A bridge built on lies and deceit?" another elder mocked. "You are nothing but a threat to our kind, a harbinger of doom."

Despair threatened to consume me. Was this all I was destined to be? A pariah in both worlds, ostracized for the very essence of who I was?

But then, I remembered the faces of the fae children, their curiosity replacing fear as I spoke of understanding. I remembered the whispers, not just of dissent, but also of hope, of a yearning for connection.

Drawing strength from those memories, I lifted my chin, my gaze unwavering. "I won't apologize for who I am," I said, my voice filled with newfound conviction. "But I choose not to be your enemy. Choose peace, and I will walk beside you. Choose fear, and I will stand against you, not as a Fae-Touched, but as Lyra, a daughter of this coven, a protector of my kind."

The chamber fell silent once more, the weight of my words hanging heavy in the air. Aric's gaze locked onto mine, scrutinizing, searching for weakness, for deceit. But all he saw was determination, a reflection of the fire burning within.

Finally, he spoke, his voice gruff but surprisingly devoid of the earlier animosity. "You walk a dangerous path, child," he said. "But perhaps there is truth in your words. Tell us more of this unrest, of these whispers."

Relief washed over me, a fragile hope battling the lingering suspicion. Maybe, just maybe, there was a chance for understanding, a path towards mending the fractured relationship between fae and vampires.

As I shared my experiences in Elyria, the whispers I'd heard, the alliances I'd forged, the seeds of doubt began to bloom within the chamber. The Elders remained cautious, their mistrust deeply ingrained, but a flicker of curiosity shone in their eyes.

By the time dawn painted the sky with streaks of crimson, an uneasy truce had settled. Aric agreed to consider my warnings, to send his own emissaries to investigate the rumblings within the fae realm. It wasn't the complete acceptance I'd hoped for, but it was a start.

Leaving the crypt, the first rays of sunlight warming my face, I knew my journey was far from over. The path between two worlds remained treacherous, riddled with suspicion and fear. But I wouldn't falter. Armed with empathy, fueled by hope, and guided by the ever-present whispers, I would continue to walk the tightrope, forging connections, building bridges, proving that even in the darkest corners, a single spark of understanding could ignite a fire of lasting peace.

Chapter Twelve

I crouched in the shadows, my heart pounding a frantic rhythm against my ribs. Across from me, shrouded in darkness, sat the very person I'd sworn to bring down - the vampire hunter, Edgar.

He hadn't changed much since our last encounter. The same haunted eyes, the same scarred hands that gripped a silver-bladed dagger, his weapon glinting menacingly in the moonlight. Yet, tonight, there was a different aura around him, an unsettling mix of desperation and grudging respect.

"You came," he rasped, his voice rough with disuse.

"Why?" I countered, my voice barely above a whisper. "After everything you've done?"

He chuckled, a harsh, humorless sound. "Desperate times call for desperate measures, Fae-Touched. And let's be honest, we have a common enemy - Morwen."

His words sent a shiver down my spine. An alliance with the very person who'd hunted me, who'd fueled the flames of fear and prejudice against my kind? It seemed unthinkable, yet the desperation in his voice resonated with a chilling truth.

"What makes you think I trust you?" I challenged, my gaze unwavering.

"Trust is a luxury we can't afford," he retorted, his eyes locking onto mine. "But hear me out. Morwen's playing a dangerous game. She claims to be an ally of the vampires, yet she whispers secrets to the fae, fanning the flames of dissent. Her motives are as murky as the shadows themselves."

My mind raced. His words echoed Morwen's cryptic pronouncements, her veiled agendas, the whispers of manipulation I'd heard within Elyria. Could there be truth to his accusations?

"What proof do you have?" I demanded, suspicion gnawing at my gut.

Edgar reached into his cloak, pulling out a worn scroll, its edges singed and brittle. He tossed it towards me, the parchment unfurling at my feet. As I picked it up, the moonlight revealed faded script, ancient symbols dancing across the page.

"An excerpt from the prophecy," he explained, his voice tight. "Hidden within the Fae Palace, stolen by an informant loyal to the truth. It speaks of a queen who will twist the prophecy, who will use the Fae-Touched as a pawn in her own power play."

My breath hitched. The words on the scroll mirrored the whispers I'd heard, the anxieties festering within both communities. Was Morwen truly playing us all, manipulating events for her own gain?

"Why are you telling me this?" I asked, my voice barely audible. "Why not expose her to the vampires?"

He scoffed. "They're blinded by their own prejudices, deaf to any voice that questions their alliance with Morwen. But you, Fae-Touched, you walk between both worlds. You have the power to see what they cannot."

His words held a grain of truth. I had witnessed the fear, the suspicion, on both sides. But could I trust a man whose hands were stained with the blood of my kind?

Hesitantly, I studied the scroll, the cryptic symbols burning into my memory. A part of me wanted to dismiss it as another ploy, another attempt to sow discord. But another part, the part attuned to the whispers, to the hidden currents beneath the surface, sensed a sliver of truth.

"What do you want from me?" I asked, my voice laced with caution.

Edgar met my gaze, his expression grim. "Help me expose Morwen's true motives. Unmask her lies and unite both vampires and fae against her manipulation. Together, we can prevent a war fueled by fear and ignorance."

His words seemed fantastical, a desperate hope in the face of an overwhelming darkness. But as I looked into his haunted eyes, I saw a flicker of something genuine, a desperation born not from malice, but from a misguided sense of justice.

Silence stretched between us, thick with the weight of the decision before me. Could I trust this man, forge an alliance with my sworn enemy, all on the basis of a cryptic scroll and a shared fear of manipulation?

Taking a deep breath, I met his gaze, my voice firm despite the tremor in my heart. "Alright, Edgar," I said. "Let's see what secrets the shadows hold."

A flicker of surprise crossed his face, quickly replaced by a grim determination. "Then let's begin," he said, his voice echoing in the silence of the night.

We spent the next few hours poring over the scroll, deciphering the ancient symbols, piecing together the fragments of Morwen's hidden agenda. Edgar, despite his gruff exterior, possessed a surprising depth of knowledge about.

Chapter Thirteen

"Ready?" he whispered, his voice barely audible above the hum of the portal.

I swallowed, my throat dry with apprehension. This was the moment of truth, the culmination of our uneasy alliance. Trusting Edgar was a gamble, but Morwen's cryptic pronouncements and the whispers of manipulation painted a chilling picture. We had to see this through.

"Lead the way," I replied, my voice laced with steely resolve.

With a nod, Edgar stepped through the portal, his form dissolving into tendrils of emerald light. I followed suit, the shimmering energy engulfing me before depositing me in a hidden chamber within the heart of the Fae Palace.

The air crackled with magic, heavy with secrets. Ornate tapestries depicting ancient battles adorned the walls, their vibrant colors dulled by time and shadow. In the center stood Morwen, her emerald eyes glowing with an otherworldly intensity.

Beside her stood Aric, his usually stoic expression clouded with confusion. His gaze met mine, a flicker of betrayal shimmering in its depths. He knew. He must have seen through Edgar's deception, understood the hunter's true purpose.

Morwen turned, her gaze sweeping over us, a knowing smile playing on her lips. "Lyra," she said, her voice a melodic chime. "And a most unexpected guest."

Edgar stepped forward, his voice devoid of fear. "The jig is up, Morwen. Your game of manipulation ends now."

Morwen tilted her head, amusement sparkling in her eyes. "Manipulation? My dear Edgar, you mistake my actions for foresight. I merely ensure the prophecy unfolds as destiny intended."

"Destiny orchestrated by you?" Edgar scoffed. "Don't play coy, Queen. We know your true intent - to exploit the war, to solidify your power over both realms using the Fae-Touched as your pawn."

The air crackled with tension. Aric shifted, his hand hovering near his sword hilt. Betrayal warred with loyalty in his eyes, the conflict tearing at him.

Morwen's smile faltered, replaced by a chilling glint of anger. "Foolish mortals," she hissed. "You overestimate your understanding. The prophecy speaks of unity, not through peace, but through dominance. And I, the rightful ruler, shall guide both vampires and fae towards their predetermined fate."

Her words shattered the last vestiges of my skepticism. Morwen wasn't an ally; she was the architect of the very conflict she claimed to want to prevent. The whispers hadn't lied.

"You used me," I whispered, hurt and anger battling within me. "You manipulated the whispers, twisted the prophecy to serve your own agenda."

Morwen laughed, a chilling sound that echoed through the chamber. "You were a useful tool, Fae-Touched. But your purpose is served. Now, witness the dawn of my reign!"

With a wave of her hand, she unleashed a torrent of emerald energy, slamming into Edgar and knocking him back. Panic surged through me, yet before I could react, Aric moved.

His sword flashed, deflecting Morwen's attack with surprising agility. Confusion morphed into determination in his eyes. He wouldn't be a pawn in her twisted game either.

A fierce battle erupted, magic clashing against steel. Edgar, fueled by righteous fury, fought with surprising skill, while Aric, torn between loyalty and betrayal, moved with a desperate grace.

I couldn't just stand by. Drawing on the raw magic within, I conjured illusions, disorienting Morwen, creating openings for Edgar and Aric to press their attack. The chamber became a whirlwind of light and energy, the tremors shaking the very foundation of the palace.

But Morwen was formidable. Her power, fueled by centuries of manipulation and ambition, was immense. Slowly, she pushed back, forcing Edgar and Aric onto the defensive. Despair threatened to consume me.

Then, I remembered the whispers, the stories of ancient alliances, of forgotten bonds between vampires and fae. Memories flashed before me - not of hatred and fear, but of cooperation, of mutual respect.

With newfound resolve, I focused my magic, not on attack, but on connection. I wove tendrils of empathy, reaching out to both Aric and Edgar, reminding them of the shared future they once envisioned, a future Morwen sought to destroy.

The energy shifted. An unseen force, fueled by shared yearning and forgotten promises, pulsed through the chamber. Aric and Edgar hesitated, their attacks faltering. Morwen, sensing the change, faltered too, confusion flickering in her emerald eyes.

It was a gamble, a fragile bridge built on memories and whispers, but it held. Aric lowered his sword, his gaze locking with mine. A silent plea for understanding, for the future we both dared to hope for, shimmered within them.

Edgar, his expression grim, followed suit, the anger in his eyes replaced by a weary resignation. The battle had shifted, not through brute force, but through a shared vision, a flicker of unity born from desperation and hope.

Morwen, however, wouldn't surrender easily. Her anger flared, the air crackling with raw power. "Foolish pawns!" she shrieked, unleashing a final, devastating blast of energy.

But it was met not with resistance, but with a shimmering shield - a collective effort woven from Aric's unwavering loyalty, Edgar's begrudging respect, and my unyielding hope. The blast dispersed, its power absorbed by the fragile, yet potent, barrier of unity.

Silence descended, thick and heavy. Morwen stood alone, her eyes wide with disbelief, the illusion of absolute power finally shattered. The whispers, once fragmented and chaotic, now hummed in unison, a symphony of shared defiance, a chorus demanding a different path.

"The prophecy," I spoke, my voice ringing with newfound strength, "it doesn't speak of dominance, but of balance. You twisted its words to suit your own desires, blinded by ambition."

A tremor ran through the chamber as ancient glyphs materialized on the walls, glowing with an ethereal light. They weren't the same symbols we'd seen before, manipulated by Morwen. These were the true words of the prophecy, unveiled by the combined will of those who dared to challenge her deceit.

The words spoke of unity, not through forced dominance, but through understanding, through acceptance of differences. They spoke of a future where vampires and fae coexisted, not as pawns in a power struggle, but as equals, bound by respect and shared responsibility.

As the true prophecy pulsed with power, Morwen's form shimmered, fading into wisps of emerald light. Her reign, built on manipulation and deceit, had crumbled under the weight of truth and unity.

The journey hadn't ended. The path ahead was still fraught with challenges, the wounds of distrust deep. But in that moment, amidst the swirling energy and the echoing whispers, a seed of hope blossomed.

Edgar, his expression unreadable, offered a curt nod. "Seems we both underestimated you, Fae-Touched."

Aric, his face etched with relief, stepped forward, offering a hand. "Together," he said, his voice rough with emotion, "we can forge a new path, one guided by the true prophecy."

I grasped his hand, the warmth spreading through me, a symbol of the fragile alliance born from adversity. The whispers, no longer harbingers of fear, hummed with a new melody, a song of hope, of collaboration, of a future where the Fae-Touched wouldn't be a pawn, but a bridge, a symbol of unity, forever walking the tightrope between two destinies, now intertwined, not by manipulation, but by the shared dream of a world bathed in the light of understanding.

ABOUT THE AUTHOR

Benjamin Blakeley is no ordinary author. Sure, he crafts fantastical tales of fae and vampires, whispering secrets of magic and forgotten prophecies. But come daybreak, you might find him trekking the Inca Trail, or haggling in the vibrant souks of Istanbul, capturing the world's stories to weave into his captivating narratives.

Born under a restless star, Ben grew up on ancient myths and tales of faraway lands, whispered by nomadic storytellers. This insatiable hunger for the world's hidden wonders fueled his own adventures, leading him to explore ancient ruins, delve into forgotten libraries, and even volunteer on archaeological digs. Each experience adds a thread to the tapestry of his imagination, enriching his stories with authenticity and depth.

When not crafting worlds through words, Ben can be found exploring the wilderness, seeking inspiration in the whispers of the wind and the secrets hidden beneath rustling leaves. He believes that magic exists not just in fantastical realms, but in the very fabric of our world, waiting to be discovered by those willing to listen.

About the Publisher

Ben is a small indie author who writes near the lake during the day but at night he is dreaming of becoming the best author

www.ingramcontent.com/pod-product-compliance
Lightning Source LLC
Chambersburg PA
CBHW021323160726
47994CB00004B/1590